Goodnight, Daddy

Written by
Angela Seward

Illustrated by
Donna Ferreiro

Morning
Glory
Press

MORNING GLORY PRESS,
6595 San Haroldo Way, Buena Park, CA 90620
714/828-1998, FAX 714/828-2049
Web site http://morninggglorypress.com

Library of Congress Cataloging-in-Publication Data
Seward, Angela, 1964-
Goodnight, Daddy / written by Angela Seward; illustrated by Donna Ferreiro.
p. cm.
Summary: Eight-year-old Phoebe looks forward to a visit from her absent
father and must deal with her disappointment when "something comes up"
and he must postpone his visit.
ISBN 1-885356-71-4 (hc.) -- ISBN 1-885356-72-2 (pbk.)
[1. Fathers and daughters--Fiction.] I. Ferreiro, Donna, 1963- ill. II. Title.

PZ7.S5158 Go 2000
[E]--dc21   00-055889

First Edition
Printed and bound in China

The illustrations in this book were rendered in watercolor,
pastels, and pencil, on Arches hot press paper.
The display type was set in Cooper Bold.
The text type was set in Americana BT.

Book and jacket design by Donna Ferreiro
Production for this book by Tim Rinker, Rinker and Associates

To all children growing up in a single-parent home –
this book is for you.
- A.S.

For my parents, Meme and Harry DeMarzi,
with love and appreciation.
- D.F.

"It's late at night, and everyone in my neighborhood is asleep except me," thought Phoebe.

"Finally! Just a few hours more and I'll be the happiest girl in the world because my daddy is coming to see me!"

Phoebe was almost six the last time she saw her father, nearly two years ago. She keeps a picture of him on her nightstand, but he isn't smiling. "I'll get a new one when I see him today," she promised herself.

Phoebe stared at the picture and remembered her daddy's last phone call. She ran to the phone so fast that she nearly tripped over her feet. But no matter how quickly she raced to the phone, the time was up too soon. She barely had time to tell him about the A's on her report card.

"When are you coming to see me, Daddy?" Phoebe had said with a slight whine in her voice.

"I don't know, Sweetheart," replied her father. "Would you like Daddy to send you a doll?"

It wasn't like having him, but she said yes, she'd like a doll. She described the newest one that spoke words in English and Spanish. He hung up after he promised they'd talk more the next time and she'd get her doll soon.

The doll never came but six months later they talked a little longer, just like he promised.

He called two weeks ago to say he'd be coming. It seemed like an eternity of waiting for Phoebe. She glanced over at her pink ballerina clock on the wall. It was 2 o'clock in the morning and she was still awake.

"Uuuuuuhhhhhhh!! I can't sleep, I'm so excited," she whispered. The far away stars, glittering in their brilliance, winked knowingly down at her.

"Are you looking up at these same stars in the sky, Daddy?" Phoebe said to herself. "I hope you are because it makes me feel like I'm with you, no matter where you are. And if I say goodnight, you can hear me."

She smiled at the stars once more before turning over and rubbing her face into the soft pillow. "Goodnight, Daddy," Phoebe whispered. "See you in the morning."

Riiiiinnnng!!!!!!

Phoebe's eyes snapped open at the sound.
It was her mother's alarm clock.

"FEEEEBEEEEEE!!!," exclaimed her mother, sounding more than slightly annoyed.

"Yes, Mom?" she answered, jumping quickly from her bed and running to her mother's room. She had turned the ringer up on the clock so she could get up early.

"Oops. I forgot to tell you I did that," she said. "I wanted to get up early so Daddy wouldn't see me in my pajamas. I need everything to be soooooo perfect, Mommy," Phoebe said with a pleading look in her eyes.

Her mother looked at her, arched an eyebrow and replied, "You should have asked me, but I understand." Then she grabbed Phoebe, and tickled her until she tumbled out of bed.

After dressing in her favorite shirt, with the big, yellow, smiley face on the front, Phoebe skipped to the bathroom. She hadn't worn the shirt in two weeks.

One day her mother asked why she wasn't wearing her favorite shirt. Phoebe replied, "I'm saving it for when Daddy gets here. I want him to see how happy I am to see him."

"I hope Daddy can make it," thought Phoebe. She frowned as her tummy suddenly did a flip-flop as she remembered another time her father had promised to visit. He had called a day ahead and said he couldn't make it. Phoebe cried all day. Her mother took her out for ice cream and a walk in the park, but it wasn't enough.

Phoebe shook her head at the thought and turned off the faucet. "He hasn't called to say he's not coming so he'll be here," she thought, as she turned off the bathroom light.

Brrrrrriiinnng! Brrrriiiinnng!

The ringing phone startled her.

"Hello?" she heard her mother say. Phoebe held her breath as she listened for the next words. Then she heard her mother's tinkling laughter as she said, "I don't believe it, Alex, you ought to stop!" then more laughter.

Phoebe closed her eyes, leaned against the wall for a moment, and let out a soft, "Whew." It was just Aunt Alex. "That stupid phone! I hope it doesn't ring anymore today!" she said to herself.

She started down the stairs but stopped at the hall mirror. Checking herself from head to toe, she moved in closer. She patted and pulled on her braids that hung like long, slender ropes down her back.

People who knew her father said she had his eyes and full lips. Phoebe smiled, then raised her small hands to smooth down the yellow smiling face on her shirt, now slightly puckered from many washes.

"I'll be there bright and early," he had said with the laugh she loved to hear. "Probably before you get out of bed."

She glanced at the hall clock. It was 9:15. The time and her rumbling tummy reminded her of breakfast. She hadn't eaten much dinner the night before.

"Is breakfast ready, Mom?" she asked, taking the stairs two at a time.

"Your cereal and juice are on the table," her mother answered.

Suddenly, Phoebe heard a car pull into the driveway.

"It's him! It's Daddy, Mommy! He's here! He's here!" Phoebe squealed.

She was so excited she could hardly breathe as she raced toward the door. As she opened it, the car began backing out of the driveway and into the street.

"Daddy?" Phoebe whispered as the car pulled away.

"That wasn't him, Sweetheart," her mother said, coming up behind Phoebe and gently guiding her back into the house. "Someone was just turning around. Go back and have your breakfast."

Phoebe quickly brushed the tears from her eyes before her mother could see them, and sat down to breakfast.

"Isn't Whitney having a party today?" her mother asked.

"Yes," Phoebe answered.

"Maybe you can still make it."

"You know I can't, Mom. Daddy's coming and I have to be here," she explained.

By 11 o'clock Phoebe was tired of watching the
morning cartoons. As she picked up the remote control
and clicked off the television, the phone rang again.

"Phoebe?" her mother called. "It's for you."

Phoebe dropped her head and sighed before slowly
rising. She hoped it wasn't her father. Her feet, that
suddenly felt as if they weighed twenty-five
pounds each, dragged along the carpet.

She took the phone from her mother's hand
and mumbled, "Hullo?"

"Phoebe? Baby, it's me, Daddy."

"Dadeee??!!" she said, irritation creeping into her voice.
"You're not supposed to be on the phone, you're
supposed to be here. Why aren't you here?" she said
shifting her feet nervously from side to side.

"I know, Honey. Daddy ran into a little problem
so I won't be able to make it today. But I'll be there
tomorrow. I promise."

Phoebe felt a stinging behind her eyes. She closed them quickly, trying to hold back the tears. I'm not going to cry, she thought, pressing her lips together . . . hard.

"Phoebe? Phoebe? Are you there?" her father asked.

"Yes. I'm here, Daddy," Phoebe replied.

"Something came up, Sweetheart, and I just can't make it," he said. "I hope you understand?"

"Well . . . Daddy, it's just that I've been waiting for so long," she began. Then she hesitated, not wanting to displease him by not understanding. "I guess one more day won't matter," she ended slowly.

"That's my big girl!" his voice boomed. "I knew you'd understand."

She stared down at a crack in the wooden floor and wondered what he looked like at that moment - with his voice filled with laughter. She could only imagine because at that moment she couldn't remember anymore.

After promising once more to come tomorrow, her father said goodbye, and Phoebe slowly hung up the phone.

"Are you all right, Phoebe?" her mother asked. "Do you want to talk?"

Phoebe took a deep breath. "No, Mom. I'm OK. I think I'll go to my room for a while."

Before she turned away, her mother leaned down to give her a hug so strong that it almost bent Phoebe backwards.

They parted and Phoebe headed upstairs. As she reached the top, she turned to look down at her mother.

"No matter what happens tomorrow, Phoebe," she said. "Just remember everything, especially you, will be OK."

Phoebe nodded her head in agreement. When she reached her room, she shut the door and plopped face down on her bed. Pressing her face down into its softness she wondered whether her father would come tomorrow like he promised.

"I'm sure Daddy must care about me a little or he wouldn't call at all," she mumbled into her covers, remembering the last time he said he couldn't come.

At that moment, her mother's words, "No matter what happens tomorrow, Phoebe, you'll be OK," echoed back to her.

She flipped over on her back and stared up at the ceiling. "I really want Daddy to come and see me, but whether he comes or not, I WILL BE OK," she said out loud. She looked around her room at the ballerina clock on the wall, her dolls and books on the shelf. She'd always liked her room. It was small, but nice.

Phoebe stared at her father's picture for a moment.
"I WILL BE OKAY!!" Phoebe said again.

Then something occurred to her. How could she have forgotten? Whenever she has a problem there is always someone she can turn to. Her mother, grandparents and aunts and uncles, always shower her with love. And her pastor and school teacher, Mrs. Fitzsimmons, too. Even after the class put creepy, fake spiders in her desk drawer! She smiled at the thought. She is always surrounded by people who love her.

Suddenly she remembered the pool party. Phoebe gave a yelp, bounced off the bed. She hoped she hadn't missed all the fun.

Later that night Phoebe got ready for bed. She took her favorite shirt, with the big, yellow, smiley face, and folded it neatly before placing it in the clothes hamper. Then she said her prayers and crawled into bed.

Her mother kissed her on the cheek before saying goodnight and switching off the light.

Phoebe looked out her window at the winking stars. As she did every night, she smiled up at them and whispered, "Goodnight, Daddy." She turned over, tossed the covers over her head and fell quickly to sleep.

About the Author and Illustrator...

Angela Seward is a single mother who says she has her hands full being mommy and daddy, juggling a job, a household, and embarking on a career as a children's book author.

She was born and grew up in the small town of Smithfield, Virginia, where she enjoyed lots of reading and writing poetry and short stories. Reluctant to break family ties, she continues to live in Virginia in the city of Newport News. She works as a news assistant for entertainment at the local paper.

Angela also provides a bi-monthly newsletter for her church, and has authored several well-received parenting columns. She's a PTA mom, avid supporter of early childhood education, and a member of the local chapter of "Proud to Be a Working Mom."

Donna Ferreiro was born and raised in New York City, and she remembers always being surrounded by art and music at home and all around her. She knew at a very young age that she wanted to be creative for the rest of her life. "I can't remember a day going by without 'coloring' or creating stories with my pictures," she remembers.

At age 9, Ferreiro wrote, illustrated and stapled together her first children's book. At 14 she was accepted into the High School of Art and Design, and eight years later received a BFA from the School of Visual Arts. Both schools are in New York City. She now lives in Southern California with her husband and two children.

After more than fifteen years of designing and art directing everything from award-winning direct mail catalogs and advertisement campaigns to posters, package and product design, she says she is thrilled to be "coloring" and making stories with her pictures again. This is her first "real" children's book.

Special Section for Single Parents

Although Phoebe is a fictional character, many children today must cope with living with only one parent. You and your partner's separation, however, doesn't mean your child must separate, too.

If the absent parent has a healthy relationship with your child, continuing that relationship is important. Otherwise, your child is likely to feel abandoned.

What can you do if the other parent doesn't keep commitments with your child? Sometimes the absent parent doesn't realize how important s/he is to your son or daughter. Maria remembers how she felt in just such a situation:

As a child, I remember so well those telephone conversations, and then the anticipation and anxiety of the wait. I felt as if I was holding my breath while I counted down the minutes until his arrival.

I would become overwhelmed with the excitement of my special day and hoped he would notice how much I'd grown. Or, I'd wonder if he would realize how much I looked like him.

But, he never came.

After several disappointments, I practiced the belief of "out of sight, out of mind." I began to pretend he didn't exist.

If this is happening to your child, can you talk to the absent parent? Rather than berating him (or her) for disappointing your child, perhaps you can focus on the other parent's importance to your son or daughter. You're rearing your child, perhaps mostly by yourself, but you know how much she misses her dad (or mother).

Share with her dad her eager anticipation before a planned visit, and how disappointed she is if Dad doesn't show up as scheduled. You might let him know your child's reaction to not getting a promised toy, but be as positive as possible.

Remember that people can only change themselves. You can't change your former partner, but you may be able to help him want to work toward a closer relationship with your child.

If Dad understands how truly important he is to his child, he may be more willing to keep his commitments.

Coping with Missed Visits

If this doesn't work, and Dad persists in missing appointments, you might decide not to talk to your daughter about the promised visits, especially if she is very young. This could save her a lot of heartache. Then, if the visit does occur, it will be a nice surprise.

When the other parent cancels a visit, you're probably upset, too. Of course you don't want your child to be disappointed.

Many of us would be tempted to try to comfort our child by putting down the other parent, but this won't help. Be as positive as you can, while remaining honest, as you talk with her about her disappointment that Mommy or Daddy didn't show up again.

Trenton, a single father in Virginia, feels strongly about the importance of honesty:

I believe in honesty. If he has questions I will answer them with a loving attitude. The most important thing is to let my son know I will always be here for him and I will never let him down or put anything before him.

It's sad when my child – whom I love very much – is "stood up" by his mother at a scheduled visit. Excuse or not, it can damage his emotions that are already sensitive because of our separation. How we handle the situation can either fix it or make it worse.

When this happens, my first feelings are of anger and hurt, but, since I love my son, doing what's best for him must override my natural feelings. First I try to say something nice about his mom, but still tell him the truth — being careful not to show any anger. I have to keep in mind that he loves his mom. Then I offer to do something he likes to take his mind off things, like go to a ball game.

Of course you'll follow through on agreements you make to your children. They have to know they can depend on you.

Sharing Feelings

If you need to talk out your negative feelings about your child's other parent — and your feelings are very important, too — confide in a friend or a relative, or see a counselor. You need someone other than your child for sharing these feelings. If you tell your son his other parent is a horrible person, he's likely to think he, too, is a bad human being. After all, half of his heritage is that person.

On the other hand, if your child is disappointed by the absent parent and begins to speak of him negatively, that's okay. You need to know what is on your child's mind. Pent-up emotions can explode in other ways.

You might say, "You must be very disappointed that Dad didn't show up today. Do you want to talk about it?" Keeping communication open between the two of you can help him deal with these disappointments with his other parent.

Continue to give your child comfort, love, guidance, support, and a listening ear. Children need to be allowed to acknowledge their feelings and to express them in non-negative ways. Elaine explains:

During the seven years in which I was a single parent, my daughter, Danielle, often asked about her father. "Do I have a dad? Where is he and why doesn't he ever come to see me?"

Although we lived in the same town and he provided child support, he only saw her three or four times during her first seven years.

I explained that not all moms and dads get married when they have children. They may even have separate lives apart from each other once the child is born.

I told her that she came from a place of love and that we both loved her very much.

I reassured her that his not being around had nothing whatsoever to do with her, but with life-style choices. He wasn't ready for marriage, so we both decided it was best to go our separate ways.

Like Phoebe's mom, Elaine reassured her daughter that she was okay whether or not she had a close relationship with her father.

Importance of Time with You

Being a single parent is often financially difficult, and you may feel overworked and harried. Somehow, though, you need to provide quality time to sustain the bond you have with your child.

Working may give your child creature comforts, but it can't replace your presence and love. If you must work many hours to make ends meet, make the best of your time together. Give your children plenty of hugs and kisses. Leave little notes in special places – they'll know you're thinking about them. You can never tell children often enough how much you love them.

Reestablishing a Relationship

Perhaps your child has had very little contact with his other parent. Now Dad wants to reestablish a relationship and maybe your child isn't interested. Help his father understand that trust must be established and the wounds of past hurts allowed to heal. Dad needs to give his child time to adjust to being close again. In the end, both will benefit.

For most children, having a relationship with both parents is important, even if their parents aren't together. It may be hard for the absent parent to establish close ties with your child. It takes time, but has high payoff in satisfaction, both for the child and her parents.

Thank you to M. Clawson, T. Cornish, and E. Brooks for the important contributions you made to this section.

Other Picture Books from Morning Glory Press

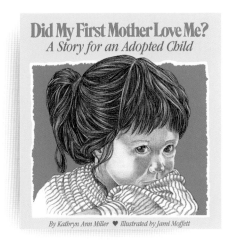

Did My First Mother Love Me?
A Story for an Adopted Child
By Kathryn Ann Miller   Illustrated by Jami Moffett

Truly a book for all Adoption Triangle members:

ADOPTEES - A wonderful story for every adopted child who wonders about his/her birthparents.

ADOPTIVE PARENTS - Guidelines for talking about adoption (9-page section, "How to Talk About Adoption with Your Child")

BIRTHPARENTS - A lovely placement gift for her child. Demonstrates her love and explains her reasons for permitting another family to raise her child.

Do I Have a Daddy?
A Story for a Single-Parent Child
By Jeanne Warren Lindsay   Illustrated by Jami Moffett

Do I Have a Daddy? has helped thousands of single mothers explain to their child why daddy is absent. A special fourteen-page section offers suggestions to single mothers, gentle advice from young mothers who've been there. 48 pp. Full color.

". . . should be required reading for single-parent families as an essential tool for building their children's self-esteem."
- Kansas City Star

¿Yo tengo papa?
1994 Spanish edition with black and white illustrations

ORDER FORM

Morning Glory Press
6595 San Haroldo Way, Buena Park, CA 90620
714/828-1998; 1-888/612-8254   Fax 714/828-2049

		Price	Total
Books for Children:			
Goodnight, Daddy			
___	1-885356-72-2	7.95	_____
___	Hardcover 1-885356-71-4	14.95	_____
Did My First Mother Love Me?			
___	0-930934-84-9	5.95	_____
___	Hardcover 0-930934-85-7	12.95	_____
Do I Have a Daddy?			
___	1-885356-63-3	7.95	_____
___	Hardcover 1-885356-62-5	14.95	_____
¿Yo tengo papá? (1993 edition, b/w illus.)			
___	Hardcover, 0-930934-83-0	12.95	_____
Books for Parents:			
Breaking Free from Partner Abuse			
___	1-885356-53-6	8.95	_____
___	Hardcover 1-885356-57-9	15.95	_____
Pregnant? Adoption Is an Option.			
___	1-885356-08-0	11.95	_____
Your Pregnancy and Newborn Journey			
___	1-885356-30-7	12.95	_____
___	Hardcover 1-885356-29-3	18.95	_____
Your Baby's First Year			
___	1-885356-33-1	12.95	_____
___	Hardcover 1-885356-32-3	18.95	_____
The Challenge of Toddlers			
___	1-885356-39-0	12.95	_____
___	Hardcover 1-885356-38-2	18.95	_____
Discipline from Birth to Three			
___	1-885356-36-6	12.95	_____
___	Hardcover 1-885356-35-8	18.95	_____
Teen Dads: Rights, Responsibilities and Joys			
___	0-930934-78-4	9.95	_____
___	Hardcover 0-930934-77-6	15.95	_____

		Price	Total
Teenage Couples: Caring, Commitment and Change			
___	0-930934-93-8	9.95	_____
___	Hardcover 0-930934-92-x	15.95	_____
Teenage Couples:Coping with Reality			
___	0-930934-86-5	9.95	_____
___	Hardcover 0-930934-87-3	15.95	_____
Will the Dollars Stretch?			
___	1-885356-12-9	6.95	_____
Novels by Marilyn Reynolds:			
___ *If You Loved Me*	1-885356-55-2	8.95	_____
___ *Baby Help*	1-885356-27-7	8.95	_____
___	Hardcover 1-885356-26-9	15.95	_____
___ *But What About Me?*	1-885356-10-2	8.95	_____
___ *Too Soon for Jeff*	0-930934-91-1	8.95	_____
___	Hardcover 0-930934-90-3	15.95	_____
___ *Detour for Emmy*	0-930934-76-8	8.95	_____
___ *Telling*	1-885356-03-x	8.95	_____
___ *Beyond Dreams*	1-885356-00-5	8.95	_____
___	Hardcover 1-885356-01-3	15.95	_____

TOTAL _____

**Add postage: 10% of total — Min., $3.50;
   15%, Canada** _____
California residents add 7.75% sales tax _____

TOTAL _____

Ask about quantity discounts, Teacher, Student Guides.
Prepayment requested. School/library purchase orders
accepted. If not satisfied, return in 15 days for refund.

NAME _____

ADDRESS _____

_____

PHONE_____ PO#_____